Little Princesses
The Sea Princess

www.**kidsatrandomhouse**.co.uk/littleprincesses

THE *Little Princesses* SERIES

The Whispering Princess
The Fairytale Princess
The Peach Blossom Princess
The Rain Princess
The Snowflake Princess
The Dream-catcher Princess
The Desert Princess
The Lullaby Princess
The Silk Princess
The Cloud Princess
The Sea Princess
The Golden Princess

Little Princesses
The Sea Princess

By Katie Chase

Illustrated by Leighton Noyes

Red Fox

Special thanks to Sue Mongredien

THE SEA PRINCESS
A RED FOX BOOK 978 0 099 48842 2

First published in Great Britain by Red Fox,
an imprint of Random House Children's Books

This edition published 2007

1 3 5 7 9 10 8 6 4 2

Series created by Working Partners Ltd
Copyright © Working Partners Ltd, 2007
Illustrations copyright © Leighton Noyes, 2007
Cover illustration by Nila Aye

The Random House Group Limited makes every effort to ensure that the papers used
in its books are made from trees that have been legally sourced from well-managed
and credibly cretified forests. Our paper procurement policy can be found at:
www.randomhouse.co.uk/paper.htm

Mixed Sources
Product group from well-managed
forests and other controlled sources
www.fsc.org   Cert no. TF-COC-2139
FSC   © 1996 Forest Stewardship Council

Set in 15/21pt Bembo Schoolbook

Red Fox Books are published by Random House Children's Books,
61–63 Uxbridge Road, London W5 5SA,
a division of The Random House Group Ltd.
Addresses for companies within the Random House Group Limited can be found at:
www.randomhouse.co.uk/offices.htm

THE RANDOM HOUSE GROUP Limited Reg. No. 954009
www.**kids**at**randomhouse**.co.uk

A CIP catalogue record for this book is available from the British Library.

Printed and bound in Great Britain by
Bookmarque Ltd, Croydon, Surrey

For Martha and Ellis Richardson,
with lots of love – *S.M.*

For Solange,
with all my love – *L.N.*

Chapter One

"Rosie, what are you doing?"

Rosie Campbell looked up from where she was lying on her bed to see her little brother Luke in the doorway. "I'm reading this," she said, holding up the joke book she'd been looking at. "Emily lent it to me at school today. Why?"

"I've got a question," Luke said. He ran in and leaped onto Rosie's bed beside her. "It's for my school project on sea creatures."

Rosie put her book down and sat up. "Go on, then," she said.

"Well," Luke began, "today, we learned about octopuses. Did you know that they squirt out black ink when they're scared?"

Rosie shook her head.

"And yesterday we learned about dolphins," Luke went on. "Mrs Lovell told us that when they're asleep, one side of their brain is still awake!"

"Cool!" Rosie replied.

"But what I really want to know is, where do all the mermaids live?" Luke asked eagerly.

Rosie smiled. "Sorry, Luke," she said. "Mermaids don't really exist. They're just in stories."

Luke shook his head stubbornly. "No, they're real," he said. "Great-aunt Rosamund said so."

Rosie frowned, wondering if her brother was trying to trick her. "When?" she asked. "Great-aunt Rosamund is in the Amazon rainforest at the moment. Didn't you see

 the postcard that
arrived yesterday?"
Rosie and Luke's
Great-aunt Rosamund
was a keen explorer,
who owned a magnificent castle in Scotland.
She had travelled all around the world,
collecting weird and wonderful souvenirs.
This time, while she was away on another
long trip, she had asked Rosie's family if they
would look after the castle for her. Rosie's
parents had agreed, so now Rosie's whole
family was living in the castle – and Rosie
had been having some wonderful adventures.

Luke had an obstinate look on his face.
"When she came to visit us last year, she
told me that she had met a mermaid
before," he told Rosie. "And she said that
the mermaid looked just like the one on
the fountain in her garden."

Rosie stared at her brother with interest. "She really said that?" she asked. "That she met a mermaid?"

"Yes!" Luke said. "And—"

But before he could say anything else, a shout floated up from downstairs. "Luke! Are you up there? Tom's on the phone for you!" called Mr Campbell.

Luke's eyes brightened. Tom was his best friend from home. "Coming, Dad!" he shouted, racing out of Rosie's bedroom at once.

"Wait!" Rosie called, but Luke had already gone. She jumped off her bed, feeling a prickle of excitement. She knew that Great- aunt Rosamund might well have made

up the mermaid story to entertain Luke, but she couldn't help hoping that there might be some truth in it. Great-aunt Rosamund had certainly met all sorts of other extraordinary people – as Rosie had been finding out for herself!

Rosie rushed out of her bedroom and down the spiral staircase. She was dying to go and see the mermaid fountain now. She had never really paid it much attention before. Great-aunt Rosamund's castle was full of the most fabulous treasures, and Rosie was always discovering new things.

She grinned as she threw on her coat and raced out of the back door into the castle grounds.

She remembered the secret message her Great-aunt Rosamund had left pinned to her pillow, telling her to "look for the Little Princesses". It had seemed like a riddle when Rosie had first read it, but then she'd found a picture of a princess on her bedside rug and had been whisked away on an amazing adventure. Since then she'd loved finding all the little princesses that were hidden around the castle.

Rosie ran across the grass. She knew that at the end of this particular stretch of lawn, there was a lavender garden with a small stone fountain at its centre.

Rosie ran through the lavender bushes until she reached the fountain. She looked at it carefully. It had once been white, but it was now weathered to grey. The bowl of the fountain had sloping sides and was carved all over with images of mermaids and mermen,

dolphins and fish. Right in the middle of the fountain, rising out of the bowl, was a statue of a young mermaid sitting on a rock.

Rosie felt her heart leap as she noticed the stone crown on top of the mermaid statue's long hair. *If she's wearing a crown, surely she must be another little princess!* Rosie thought excitedly.

Eagerly, she bobbed a curtsey and said a breathless, "Hello!" to the little mermaid.

Instantly, a gust of wind picked up from nowhere and whirled around Rosie, lifting her off her feet. She could smell the salty tang of sea air, and hear the beautiful, haunting sound of singing. Another adventure was beginning . . .

Chapter Two

Moments later, the wind set Rosie down. It was night time, and the smell of the sea filled the air. A pale full moon hung in the sky, surrounded by glittering stars, and Rosie gazed about curiously to see that she was standing on a deserted beach. The sand felt cool and damp under her bare feet, and, looking down, she saw that she was now wearing an ankle-length sleeveless dress that shimmered blue-green in the moonlight.

Rosie could still hear the same haunting melody she'd heard in the whirlwind. It seemed to be coming from the sea, so she padded across the wet sand towards some

large rocks that stood between her and
the water.

The singing was louder now, so Rosie
clambered onto the slippery rocks and gazed
out to sea. From her new vantage point,
she could see right out to the furthest rock
jutting out of the ocean. And there on the
rock, with waves splashing up all around
her, sat a beautiful mermaid, singing and
combing her hair.

Rosie gasped and stared in amazement.
From the waist up, the mermaid looked very
much like a normal girl. She wore a delicate
silver top, and was combing her auburn hair
with a curved turquoise comb that glinted
in the moonlight. But from the waist down,
where a girl would have had legs, she had
the shining, scaly tail of a fish, which
glimmered a magnificent greeny-blue.

At the sound of Rosie's gasp, the mermaid

immediately stopped singing and turned round. As her gaze met Rosie's, Rosie noticed that the mermaid's eyes shone silver like the moon.

"Are you a real human?" the mermaid asked, sounding awestruck.

"Yes," Rosie said, with a smile. "My name's Rosie."

The mermaid clapped her hands. "How exciting! Do come nearer so I can have a proper look at you."

Rosie scrambled across to the mermaid's rock and sat down next to her.

4

The mermaid stared at Rosie, seemingly drinking in every detail. Then she glanced around a little warily. "I should probably swim away, right now," she confessed. "Mer-people are supposed to remain hidden from humans at all times, but" – she grinned suddenly – "I've never met a *real* human before, so maybe I could stay for a little while . . ."

Rosie grinned back, liking the friendly mermaid at once. "Don't worry, I'm very good at keeping secrets," she assured her. "I promise I won't tell anyone that I've met you. What's your name?"

"Princess Marissa," the mermaid replied. "You can just call me Marissa, though. My mum and dad are the king and queen of the mer-people. We live in the Kingdom of Aquatica in the depths of the ocean."

"I live in a castle in Scotland," Rosie said,

"but I've come here by magic!"

The mermaid looked interested. "My grandmother used to tell me about a human girl called Rosamund who came to visit her," she said. "And *she* came by magic too! They were very good friends, and used to love exploring Aquatica together."

Rosie nodded. "That girl – Rosamund – she's my great-aunt," she explained.
Then she frowned as a thought struck her. "Wait, though. How did Rosamund manage to swim underwater with your grand-mother?"

"Well, my grandmother said that she just touched Rosamund on the forehead and then she turned into a mermaid, too," Marissa replied. She shot Rosie a thoughtful look. "Shall we try it for ourselves?"

Rosie nodded, her heart pounding with excitement, and Marissa stretched out her

hand and touched Rosie's forehead with
one finger.

All at once, Rosie felt the strangest tingling
sensation spread right through her body. The
water around the rock suddenly glowed with
a mysterious golden light, and then a wave
that sparkled with tiny flickering lights
splashed right up onto the rock, covering
Rosie's legs.

"Oh!" gasped Rosie as the cold water hit her. And then she stared in disbelief as the seawater poured off the rock once more. For there, where her legs had been only moments before, she could see a beautiful golden tail in their place. She was a mermaid!

Chapter Three

"Wow!" Rosie laughed, gazing in wonder at her shimmering tail. She couldn't take her eyes off it. Then she realized that her dress had vanished along with her legs, and she was now wearing a sparkly turquoise top.

Marissa grinned. "It works!" she exclaimed in delight. "That means you must be a true friend. My grandmother said that only if a human is pure of heart and a true friend to the mer-people, will they turn into a mer-person themselves." Then she glanced at the sky, where pink and orange streaks were beginning to appear. "The sun's going to be up soon," she said, slipping gracefully into the sea. "We need to get underwater before it's light, or we might be spotted. Come and try out your new tail, Rosie!"

Rosie slid carefully into the water next to Marissa, who was now completely submerged. Rosie held her breath and dipped beneath the surface too. To her amazement, she found that she could see perfectly well without goggles, even though the sky was only just beginning to grow light. And she could breathe easily underwater too! "I can't believe this is happening," she said in awe as a school of silvery fish swam past her eyes. "Everything is so bright and clear!

How come I can see so well, when it isn't even full daylight yet?"

Marissa pointed to her own eyes. "You have mermaid eyes now, as well as a mermaid's tail," she said, with a joyful flick of her tail. "Come on – try out your swimming skills! Let's see how fast we can go and then I will show you the Kingdom of Aquatica!"

Rosie nodded enthusiastically, pushed off with her tail and headed after Marissa.

Immediately, she found herself shooting
along the seabed at a tremendous rate,
skimming over the sand, stones and the
silvery darting fish. "Wow," she said to herself.
"This is a lot easier than front crawl!"

The ocean was alive with colour and life.
Rosie lost count of the number of different
kinds of fish she saw swimming through the
bobbly seaweed, and she gazed in delight at
the brightly coloured coral and shells lying

like treasure on the sandy seabed.

Suddenly a couple of dolphins came swerving towards them, their silvery-grey bodies moving powerfully through the water. Rosie watched them in fascination. She had never seen a real dolphin up close, although she had a poster of some dolphins on her bedroom wall back in the castle. She was about to move out of the way when she

realized that Marissa was waving to them and calling them over. "Carla! Carlos! Come and meet Rosie!"

The dolphins nosed their way over, and looked at Rosie with bright black eyes.

"Hello," the slightly larger dolphin said in a whistling sort of voice. "I'm Carlos."

"And I'm Carla," the second dolphin added, smiling.

"Hello," Rosie said, beaming back at them.

"Do you two want to play hide and seek?" Carlos asked.

"Oh, yes," Marissa said at once. "My favourite!"

"Great," Carlos said, snapping his eyes shut. "One . . . two . . . three . . ." he counted.

Carla quickly swam away, and Rosie turned to Marissa. "Where shall we hide?" she whispered. "Do you know any good places around here?"

Marissa pursed her lips in thought for a moment as she looked around. Then she pointed at a small rock, about the size of Rosie's fist, on the seabed. "We could hide behind that," she suggested.

Rosie giggled. She thought Marissa must be joking – the rock would only have hidden the smallest of fish. It certainly wasn't big enough for two mermaids to hide behind! "Maybe the coral reef, over there?" Rosie suggested instead. "It's not far and—"

But Marissa interrupted her excitedly. "I know," she whispered. "Let's not hide at all!

Carlos won't be expecting that!"

Rosie couldn't help laughing at her friend's idea. "He won't," she agreed. "But it'll be a very fast game of hide and seek that way!"

Marissa opened her mouth to reply, but just then Carlos was saying, "Nineteen . . . twenty! Coming, ready or not!"

He opened his eyes and swam straight over to them. "Found you!" he chuckled. "That was easy, Marissa." He turned to Rosie, still smiling. "It usually takes me ages to find Marissa. She's fantastic at hiding."

Marissa was looking a little confused. She frowned to herself. "What *was* I doing?" she murmured, sounding puzzled. "I don't know why I thought that not hiding would be a good idea in a game of hide and seek! How silly of me!"

"Never mind," Rosie said comfortingly. "Let's find Carla, shall we? Then maybe we could play something else."

The three of them tracked down Carla in a clump of brown seaweed a few minutes later.

"How about a game of tag?" Marissa suggested. "I'll be It. Ready? Go!"

Rosie dodged away from her new friend, pushing herself off with her tail as quickly as she could. She loved the feeling of swimming so fast, with the water rushing past her face.

This is a truly amazing adventure, she thought happily as she swam further into the ocean. I love being a mermaid! I absolutely love it!

But just as that thought floated into her head, the light seemed to dim all around her. Rosie looked up in alarm, and tried not to scream with fright. A huge shadow was darkening the water above her. A shadow with eight long tentacles. It was an enormous octopus, Rosie realized with a jolt, and it was heading straight for her.

Chapter Four

Rosie whirled around in the water, searching for her friends. "Marissa! Carla! Carlos! Watch out!" she yelled. "A massive octopus is coming!"

Marissa swam over, smiling. "Don't worry, it's only Octavius," she said reassuringly. "He's our friend."

Rosie felt her heartbeat gradually settle down, and sighed in relief. "Oh," she said. "Phew!"

Carla and Carlos nodded their heads in agreement.

"Octavius is very nice," Carla said. "Here he comes. You can meet him yourself."

The octopus gradually sank towards them, his tentacles floating around him.

"Octavius, this is my new friend, Rosie," Marissa said. "She's actually a human, and this is her first time underwater. That's why she was a bit scared of you."

The octopus let out a throaty chuckle, and held out a tentacle for Rosie to shake. "Scared of *me*?" he said, smiling. "Usually it's the other way round. *I'm* scared of *humans!*"

Rosie suddenly remembered what Luke had told her earlier. "Hello, Octavius," she said politely. "Is it true that octopuses squirt black ink when they're frightened?"

Octavius nodded his head. "That's right," he said. "And blue ink when we're sad, and pink ink when we're happy, or when we think something's funny." He winked. "Of course, most humans never get to see the pink ink, because octopuses are usually scared whenever they see humans."

"Well, there's no need to be scared of me," Rosie said, smiling up at the friendly creature.

"Octavius, we were just playing tag," Marissa told him. "Would you like to join in?"

"I'd love to," Octavius replied.

"But you can't use all eight of your tentacles," Carla put in promptly, "or none of us will stand a chance!"

Octavius laughed. "All right, I'll just use these two," he said, waggling the two central tentacles in front of him.

They were just about to begin the game when the temperature around them suddenly plummeted, and the sea became cold. "Oh, no!" Marissa exclaimed fearfully. "We'll have to go. The Sea Hag is coming! The water always becomes icy whenever she's nearby," she explained to Rosie. "Come on!"

"Quick!" urged Carla, diving ahead. "This way!"

Rosie swam after her new friends as quickly as she could, feeling nervous. The others all seemed to be very afraid of this Sea Hag. Rosie figured she must be someone very scary.

As soon as they were a safe distance away, and the water had warmed up again, Rosie turned to Marissa. "What's so awful about the Sea Hag?" she asked curiously. "And who is she?"

Marissa gave a shudder. "She's an old mermaid who lives in a cave on the fringes of the kingdom," she told Rosie. "It's said that she likes to collect things, and if she catches anyone, she keeps them in her cave for ever! That's why nobody in the kingdom ever goes near her if they can help it."

Rosie felt a shiver run down her back. She definitely didn't want to meet the Sea Hag!

Carla looked across at Carlos. "We should go," she said. "Mum will be worried if we don't come home soon, especially with the Sea Hag about."

"Goodbye," Rosie said to the dolphins. "It was fun playing with you."

Carla and Carlos smiled and waved their flippers at Rosie as they swam away.

Octavius waved at the dolphins with several of his tentacles, then turned back to Marissa and Rosie. "We could go to my den," he suggested. "We should be safe there."

"Good idea," Marissa said. "And Rosie might be able to tell us more about your treasures, too! They *are* from the human world, after all."

"What kind of treasures?" Rosie asked, imagining gold and silver trinkets in a treasure chest.

But Octavius was already drifting away. "Come and see," he said. "It's this way."

Rosie followed Octavius and Marissa to a

huge sunken ship that was lying on the
bottom of the ocean. It looked like an old
Spanish galleon that had clearly been very
grand in its day, but it now had broken masts
and rotting timbers, and it lay on its side.
Rosie couldn't help wondering how long the
ship had been down there as she swooped
between the fallen masts.

"Come and see the enchanted wall,"
Octavius said, beckoning Rosie with a

tentacle. "It's one of my finest treasures – and *very* magical. You see, it changes every time somebody looks at it." He led her into a cabin. The ceiling was partly rotted away above them, and the furniture had all gone, but on one wall there still hung a huge mirror which, astonishingly, remained unbroken.

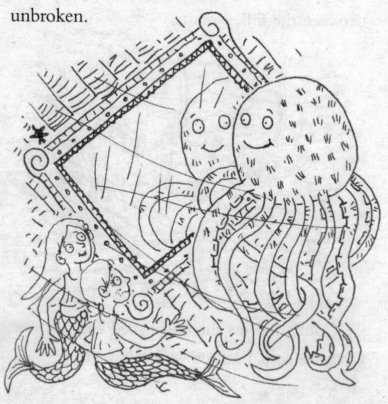

Octavius bobbed cautiously in front of the mirror then dodged away as he saw his own reflection. "There! Did you see that?" he asked Rosie in a whisper. "When I look at it, an octopus appears. When Marissa looks in it, a mermaid just like her appears. But they never speak to us. I think they might be shy. Do they behave the same way in your world?"

Rosie tried to stifle a giggle. It wasn't quite the "treasure" she'd been expecting! "It's called a mirror," she told Octavius. "Humans use it to check how they look. What you see in the mirror is your reflection — it's like a picture of yourself."

Marissa had swum up and was listening intently. "Why would anyone want to check how they look?" she asked.

"Well, when you've brushed your hair, you can look in the mirror and make sure it's how you want it to be," Rosie explained. "And when you—"

"Ssshh!" Octavius interrupted suddenly. "I think someone's coming!" He swam up through the cabin roof, then returned, looking tense. "Humans," he whispered urgently. "And they're coming this way!"

Chapter Five

Through the rotten old beams of the cabin
ceiling, Rosie could see dark shapes
approaching. Divers coming down to look
at the shipwreck, she guessed.

"Ooh, yes, there they are!" Marissa said
breathlessly. "Lots of them. How exciting!"

Octavius shot her an agonized look. "We'll
have to be quiet," he reminded the princess.
"We mustn't let them see us or hear us!"

"I might just say a quick hello," Marissa
said dreamily, floating upwards.

Octavius stretched out a tentacle and
grabbed her hand, stopping her from
swimming any further. "What are you

doing?" he hissed anxiously.

"Shouldn't we be hiding, Marissa?" Rosie put in. "I thought mer-people were supposed to stay away from humans."

Marissa had a faraway look in her eyes. "Yes, but *you're* such a nice human, Rosie," she said, "I'd really like to get to know some other ones, too."

"No, definitely not," Octavius said, before Rosie could reply. "Princess Marissa, it could be dangerous. We must hide at once!"

Marissa blinked suddenly and shook her head. She looked confused for a moment, and then her face cleared. She glanced up at the divers and nodded decisively. "Yes, we must," she said. "Of course we must! I can't believe I was thinking of doing anything else. How silly of me!"

"Quick, then," Octavius said, swimming towards one of the adjoining cabins. "Come

this way before they see us!"

Rosie and Marissa followed Octavius, then pressed their backs against the wall of the new cabin and kept very still. But Rosie could hear the divers drawing nearer and nearer. She bit her lip anxiously. If she and Marissa were discovered, she knew it would mean big trouble for the mer-people of Aquatica. A diver paddled just a few metres above their heads.

"Maybe we should try to get away?" Rosie hissed nervously.

Octavius nodded. "Change of plan," he whispered. "Hiding here is too risky. I'll swim up to the divers and squirt black ink at them to block their view. That way, you two can swim away without being seen."

"Thank you," Rosie whispered, hugging the brave octopus.

"Thanks, Octavius," Marissa added. "Come on, Rosie. Let's get out of here!"

Rosie and Marissa crept out of the cabin and down to the seabed, ready to dart away along the sand.

"There he goes!" Rosie hissed, seeing their courageous friend floating up through the water.

Seconds later, the sea above them turned black, as Octavius's ink spread all around.

"Now!" Marissa cried, tugging Rosie by the hand and swimming away from the ship. "Faster, Rosie – as fast as you can!"

Rosie pushed off with her tail and felt herself fly forwards through the water. She was relieved to be leaving the ship behind but concerned about Octavius. "Will Octavius be all right?" she called to Marissa.

Marissa nodded. "He'll be fine," she said confidently. "The ink will disguise him too and he'll be able to get away. He's used to the ink, but the divers aren't."

Rosie followed Marissa as she swam swiftly through the water, past coral reefs and shoals of fish. She began to feel disorientated as Marissa took them deeper and deeper into the ocean, veering sharp left past a whole pod of dolphins, and then twisting her way through a dark seaweed forest.

Finally they reached a pair of sparkling golden gates and the princess turned and smiled at Rosie. "Here we are at last," she said. "This is the Kingdom of Aquatica. Welcome!"

Marissa led Rosie through the gates and along a wide curving path that seemed to be made of glittering green sea glass. On either side of the path were tall, elegant coral buildings, with shell roofs and windowsills, and front gardens filled with colourful sea anemones. Rosie saw two little mermaids playing in a garden, and another mermaid waved at her from a window.

"This is lovely!" she said, gazing around in delight. "What a beautiful place to live!"

Marissa smiled. "Wait until you see the palace," she said. "We'll get a glimpse of it any second."

Rosie gasped as they followed the green path round a corner. In front of her a spectacular building had appeared, carved from glittering turquoise stone. It had turrets made from shining mother-of-pearl, and strings of pearls edged every window. "It's

like something out of a fairytale," Rosie
breathed, still staring. "An underwater
fairytale!"

Marissa took her by the arm. "Come on,"
she said proudly. "I'll show you inside."

Chapter Six

Marissa led Rosie
through a set of
silvery double
doors that were guarded
by two sea horses.
The sea horses
bowed respectfully
as the two mermaids
swam through, and Marissa called out a
cheerful greeting.

Rosie followed Marissa down a grand
hallway that had gleaming silver walls and
a turquoise ceiling. Portraits of different
generations of royal mermaids lined the

walls. As she swam past, Rosie realized that each portrait was made up of thousands of tiny shells, painstakingly stuck down into a mosaic, and she couldn't resist stopping to marvel at them.

"Come on, Rosie," Marissa called from further down the hallway. "We'll go to the throne room first. Mum and Dad might be in there. I can't wait for you to meet them!"

Marissa led Rosie along a series of corridors until they reached a huge golden door which had a beautiful ruby-coloured shell for a doorknob. Marissa pushed open the door and swam a little way inside. Then she turned back to Rosie with a grin. "Here they are! Rosie, come and meet Mum and Dad – the King and Queen of Aquatica!"

Rosie's eyes widened as she swam into the grand throne room. The walls were made of red and gold sea glass that glittered in the light, and at the far end were two huge golden thrones, inlaid with all sorts of colourful jewels. On the thrones sat the king and queen, talking eagerly to one of their servants. The king wore a golden crown with a huge diamond set in the middle of it, and the queen had a crown set with a twinkling ruby.

Rosie frowned slightly as she and Marissa approached. For a moment she was reminded of something. Something about a crown . . . She thought hard, but the next moment she was being introduced to the king and queen, and the memory slipped away.

"Mum, Dad," Marissa was saying, "this is Rosie, my new friend. She's a human, and guess what? Remember Grandmother's friend Rosamund? Well, Rosie is Rosamund's great-niece!"

Rosie dropped into a curtsey as the king and queen gazed at her. "Very nice to meet you," she said politely.

"Nice to meet you, too," the queen smiled.

"Yes, indeed," the king added happily. Then he glanced back to the servant he and the queen had been speaking to. "So, is that all clear?"

The servant, a dark-haired merman in a silver waistcoat, swept a bow. "Ten thousand stones to be delivered to the palace by tomorrow. I'll see to it at once, Your Majesties." And with another bow, he darted out of the throne room.

Marissa wrinkled her nose in surprise. "Ten thousand stones? Are you having something built?" she asked.

The queen nodded, beaming. "Your father has had the most wonderful idea!" she declared.

"I've ordered a royal swimming pool to be built!" the king explained.

Marissa beamed. "That's great!" she cried happily. "Actually it's better than great, it's *fantastic*!"

Rosie stared from Marissa to the king and queen in bewilderment. She wondered if she was missing something. A swimming pool under the sea? Why would anybody go to all the trouble of building a swimming pool when they already lived in the water? She quickly forced a smile onto her face as Marissa grinned at her. She didn't want to seem rude, so she nodded and smiled and tried to look as if she thought it was a wonderful plan too.

The king got off his throne and stretched out a hand to the queen. "Come, my dear," he said. "We need to pick a site for our new pool." He turned back to Marissa and Rosie. "Do feel free to join us, once you've shown our guest around the palace, Marissa."

The king and queen swam out of the throne room, leaving Rosie and Marissa alone. "Won't it be fun to swim in the royal swimming pool, once it's finished?" Marissa said brightly.

Rosie couldn't hold back her confusion any longer. "Marissa, I don't understand," she confessed. "Why do mer-people need a swimming pool when they live in the sea?"

Marissa's smile faded. She blinked and shook her head, just as Rosie had seen her do during the game of hide and seek, and in

Octavius's den. "You're right," she said to Rosie in a trembling voice. "You're absolutely right. It is quite the silliest thing I've ever said. And, even worse, this is the *third* silly thing I've said today. Something is very wrong." Marissa put a hand to her head and patted her hair. Instantly all the colour drained from her face and she gasped in dismay. "Oh, no!" she cried. "It's gone!"

Chapter Seven

"Your crown!" Rosie said at once. She'd
known something was missing as soon as
she'd seen the king and queen wearing
their crowns. That was what she'd half
remembered – that the mermaid in the
stone fountain had been wearing a crown,
whereas Marissa hadn't.

"*That's* why I've been saying such silly
things all day!" Marissa exclaimed, looking
aghast. "It's because I've lost the crown, and
the crown holds the Pearl of Wisdom!"

"The Pearl of Wisdom?" Rosie echoed.
"What's that?"

Marissa put her head in her hands. "Each

member of our royal family has a crown set with a special jewel," came her muffled voice. She looked up 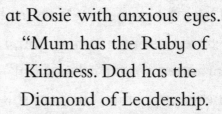 at Rosie with anxious eyes. "Mum has the Ruby of Kindness. Dad has the Diamond of Leadership. And I have 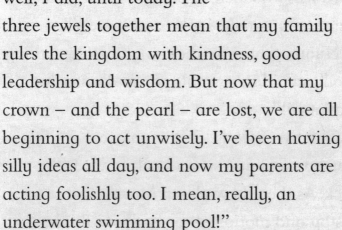 the Pearl of Wisdom – well, I did, until today. The three jewels together mean that my family rules the kingdom with kindness, good leadership and wisdom. But now that my crown – and the pearl – are lost, we are all beginning to act unwisely. I've been having silly ideas all day, and now my parents are acting foolishly too. I mean, really, an underwater swimming pool!"

Rosie put an arm around her friend's

shoulders. "Don't worry," she said. "I'll help you find your crown. Where did you last see it?"

"I remember taking it off when I was combing my hair," Marissa said slowly. Then she gasped. "Of course! I was so excited about meeting you, I must have forgotten to put it back on!" She gave Rosie a sheepish smile. "It must still be on the rock."

"Let's go back to the rock right away, then," Rosie said.

Marissa nodded. "I have to get it back before my parents make any more silly decisions, otherwise they might do something really stupid that would mean disaster for Aquatica!"

The two friends left the palace immediately and swam back towards the rock. As they drew closer, Marissa came to a stop and motioned for Rosie to do the same. "Here we are," she said in a low voice.

"We need to be really careful now because
it's day time. We mustn't be seen." She poked
her head out of the water cautiously and
looked around. Then she ducked down to
speak to Rosie. "It's safe. Nobody's on the
beach. Come on!"

Rosie followed Marissa as she pulled
herself up onto the large grey rock. The
beach was bathed in sunshine now, but
still quite deserted.

"Here's my comb," Marissa said. "But my crown isn't here."

"Maybe a wave knocked it off the rock," Rosie suggested. "Let's hunt around on the seabed."

"Good thinking," Marissa agreed, looking anxious.

Rosie and Marissa both plunged back into the water and began searching all around the rock, turning over the sand and stones with their fingers in hopes of seeing a glint of gold. After a while, though, it was quite clear that the crown wasn't there.

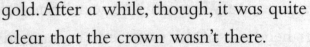

Marissa looked devastated. "This is awful!" she cried, biting her lip. "My parents trusted me with the Pearl of Wisdom – and I've lost it! What are we going to do?"

Rosie tried to comfort her. "It must be around here *somewhere*," she said. "It can't have just vanished."

At that moment a turtle who'd been snoozing on the seabed nearby opened his eyes. "What's all this noise about?" he asked grumpily. "You've just woken me up!"

"Sorry," Rosie said. She swam closer to the turtle. "We're looking for Princess Marissa's crown. Have you seen it anywhere?"

The turtle yawned. "Yes," he replied. "I've seen it. And I'll tell you where it went, too — but only if you promise to go away and leave me in peace."

"We promise," Rosie and Marissa chorused at once.

The turtle gave another great yawn. "The Sea Hag took it," he told them, and then he shut his eyes again.

Rosie stared at Marissa in horror. "The Sea Hag!" she echoed. "Oh, no! What do we do now?"

Marissa looked determined. "I'll have to find the Sea Hag and ask for my crown back," she said. "You wait here, Rosie, and I'll be as quick as I can."

Rosie shook her head. "There's no way I'm

going to let you face the Sea Hag alone," she
said staunchly. "I'm coming with you – and
that's that!"

Chapter Eight

"Are you sure, Rosie?" Marissa asked.

Rosie nodded. "Absolutely," she said,
slipping her arm through Marissa's. "You
must be having another silly idea if you
think I'd let you go alone."

Marissa smiled gratefully. "Thank you,"
she said, and pointed downwards. "Her
cave is right at the bottom of the ocean,"
she told Rosie.

Rosie looked down to where her friend
was pointing. She couldn't see the seabed
from where they were, only endless blue.
"Come on, then," she said, preparing herself.
"Let's go."

Down the friends swam, and down. The water became colder and murkier as they descended. Before long the temperature had dropped so severely that Rosie's teeth began to chatter.

"Nearly there," Marissa muttered with a shiver. "It's just up ahead."

At last Marissa stopped in front of a cave, and Rosie swam to her side. The cave entrance was covered by two curtains that seemed to have been

woven from green seaweed. Rosie and Marissa each took hold of one curtain and pulled it aside.

"Come on," Rosie whispered. She was trying to sound brave and encouraging, but her heart was beating so fast she was surprised Marissa couldn't hear it.

They slipped past the curtains and into the cave, which was dimly lit by ice crystals that hung from the ceiling. At the back of the cave was a door made out of driftwood, with an icy knocker shaped like a shark.

Marissa reached out nervously, lifted the knocker and let it fall. The two friends huddled together while they waited.

Moments later the door was flung open, and the Sea Hag stood in the doorway. She had wild white hair and a scowl on her face. Rosie could feel coldness coming off her in waves and she shivered. The Sea Hag was

very scary. "What do you want?" she snarled. "Why are you knocking on my door? Trying to play a trick on me, are you?"

"N-no," stammered Marissa. "I am Marissa, Princess of Aquatica, and I was wondering . . . I mean . . . I think you may have something that belongs to me. Could I have it back now, please?"

The Sea Hag's scowl deepened. "I have nothing that belongs to you," she said. "Everything in my cave belongs to me!" And with that, she slammed the door in the girls' faces.

Marissa flinched as the wooden door crashed against its frame. "That didn't go very well," she said, looking anxious.

"We can't give up now, though," Rosie said firmly. And before she had time to change her mind, she reached up and banged the door-knocker herself.

The door flew open again, and this time the Sea Hag looked even angrier than before. "Now what?" she thundered.

"We know you've got the crown," Rosie said, trying to keep her voice steady. "And we're not leaving until you give it back." She paused and then, for good measure, she added, "The Kingdom of Aquatica depends on it!"

"We promise it's not a trick," Marissa added desperately.

The Sea Hag stared at them for a few moments. She seemed to be thinking hard. "Very well," she said at last. "You'd better come in."

She turned and swam further into the cave, leaving the door open behind her. Rosie smiled nervously at Marissa and then the two friends followed the Sea Hag into the main chamber of the cave.

As they swam through another set of seaweed curtains, Rosie couldn't help but let out a gasp. The large room they'd just entered was absolutely crammed with treasure! Rosie stared around at golden necklaces, strings of pearls, silver plates, gold coins and caskets of jewels with the gems spilling out of them: sapphires, rubies, diamonds, emeralds and other glittering

stones Rosie had never even seen before.

The Sea Hag sat down on a chair made from a giant scallop shell. She pulled out a pair of long coral knitting needles that had some knitted green seaweed dangling from them, and used them to point upwards. "Is that the crown you were talking about?" she asked.

Rosie looked up and saw, up on a high shelf, a golden crown set with a large creamy-white pearl.

"Yes," Marissa said eagerly, her eyes on the crown, too. "Yes, that's it!"

The Sea Hag was knitting busily. "I found it abandoned on the seabed," she said in an icy voice, as her coral needles clattered away. "That's where I find most of my treasures. I feel sorry for them. They are lost and forgotten about." She glared at Marissa and Rosie. "Just as I am."

"But I didn't *mean* to leave my crown behind," Marissa said desperately. "And I need it back!"

"Everything needs to be looked after," the Sea Hag went on, ignoring Marissa. "Even old, forgotten things. But it seems that the mer-people are careless with their things and with their people. Especially with people like me!" Her eyes glittered with angry tears. "And because of that, I say this to you: that the crown is mine now. I found it. And I am not going to give it back!"

Chapter Nine

Marissa looked at the Sea Hag in anguish. "You already have so many beautiful things, why do you need my crown, too?" she asked.

"Without the crown, the princess and her parents will lose their wisdom," Rosie put in. "The Kingdom of Aquatica is in danger!"

The Sea Hag snorted. "Why should I care about Aquatica, when Aquatica has never cared about me?" she asked bitterly. She looked down at her lap, and a sad expression came over her face. "Nobody even knows my *name*," she said. "They just call me 'the Sea Hag'. What sort of a name is that?" She sighed sorrowfully. "Nobody ever comes to visit me. And whenever I try to speak to the other mer-people, they just swim away because I make them cold."

Rosie was starting to feel a bit sorry for the lonely Sea Hag. "Well, *I* would like to know your name," she said softly, taking a step forwards. "My name is Rosie," she added encouragingly.

There was a long silence, then, "Myrtle," the Sea Hag said shyly. "My name is Myrtle."

"Well, Myrtle," Marissa said, "on behalf of all Aquatica, I would like to apologize. The mer-people *have* been unfriendly to you, but only because we were all . . . well, scared of you."

Myrtle's eyebrows shot up. "Scared?" she echoed. "Of me? Why?"

"Because . . . because everyone says that you collect mer-*people* as well as treasure," Marissa said hesitantly. "And that you never let them go."

Myrtle stared at Marissa in disbelief. "They really say that? That I collect *people*?" she asked.

Marissa and Rosie both nodded.

"What utter nonsense!" Myrtle exclaimed. She shook her head as if she couldn't believe her ears. "What codswallop! Why ever would I want to collect *people*? Where would I put them? Honestly!" She looked over at Rosie and Marissa, and seemed to notice for the first time that they were both shivering. "Would you like a jumper or a shawl to keep warm?" she asked, suddenly sounding a little kinder.

"Y-y-yes please," Rosie said, through chattering teeth.

"That would be great," Marissa agreed.

Myrtle opened a wooden chest to reveal
piles of knitted jumpers, shawls and scarves,
all made from green, white and blue
seaweed. "Here," she said, passing the girls
a shawl each. "You should have said that
you were cold."

"Thank you," Rosie said, wrapping her
shawl around her shoulders. She'd expected it
to feel unpleasantly cold and slimy, but
actually it was wonderfully warm and snug.

"It's lovely," she said to Myrtle with a smile.

"*Really* lovely," Marissa agreed, snuggling into hers. "Thank you, Myrtle."

The tips of Myrtle's ears turned pink with the praise. "I do my best," she said modestly. "It's just a shame I don't have any prettier colours to knit with. I only have blue, green and white seaweed."

All of a sudden, Rosie had a brilliant idea. "Myrtle, if we could get you some brightly coloured seaweed, do you think you might swap it for Marissa's crown?" she asked eagerly.

Myrtle immediately looked suspicious again. "You're trying to trick me, aren't you?" she asked. "I knew it! Well, you won't fool me. I know every inch of this kingdom. The only seaweed that grows around here is green, blue and white."

Rosie smiled. "Ahh, but what if we could

bring you some pink seaweed, would we
have a deal?" she asked.

"Rosie, what are you—?" Marissa hissed,
but Rosie gave her a reassuring wink.

"Trust me," she whispered.

Myrtle still looked dubious. "I saw that
wink, young lady," she snapped. "I don't
know what funny business you're planning,
but—"

"No funny business," Rosie assured her.
"I promise. And you'll be able to see the pink
seaweed for yourself before you have to
swap."

"Very well," Myrtle said cautiously. "It's
a deal."

"One last thing," Rosie said. "May we have some of your white seaweed, please?"

Myrtle handed over a large bundle of white seaweed, her bright eyes curious.

"Thank you," Rosie said, tucking it under her arm. "We'll be back as soon as possible. Come on, Marissa, we have work to do!"

Rosie and Marissa swam out of Myrtle's cave. "What are you plotting?" Marissa asked as soon as they were out of earshot.

Rosie grinned at her and held up the white seaweed. "We need to find Octavius," she said, "and ask him to squirt some of his ink over this to turn it bright pink!"

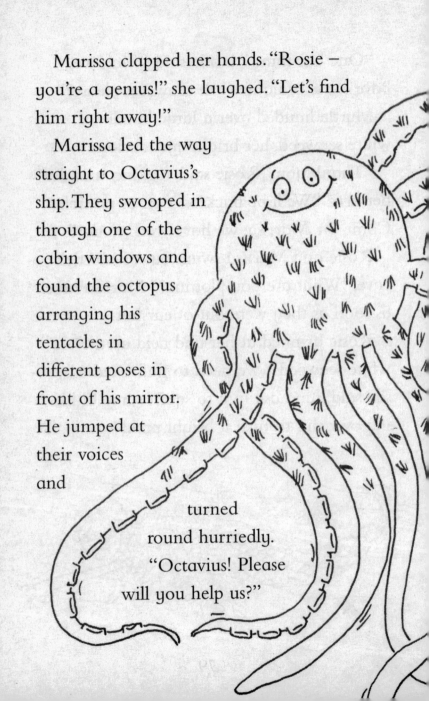

Marissa clapped her hands. "Rosie — you're a genius!" she laughed. "Let's find him right away!"

Marissa led the way straight to Octavius's ship. They swooped in through one of the cabin windows and found the octopus arranging his tentacles in different poses in front of his mirror. He jumped at their voices and

turned round hurriedly. "Octavius! Please will you help us?"

Marissa asked. "The future of Aquatica depends on it!"

She and Rosie told him the whole story of how Marissa had lost her crown and the Pearl of Wisdom, and how Rosie had struck a deal with Myrtle to get the crown back.

"So, all we need is for you to squirt some pink ink on the seaweed – and all our problems are solved!" Rosie finished hopefully.

Octavius stared at the white seaweed, and his face crumpled in despair. "I'm really sorry," he said, "but I simply don't have enough pink ink to do that." He looked positively heartbroken at the thought of letting Marissa down. "Is there no other way to get the crown back?" he asked hopefully.

Rosie stared at Octavius in surprise for a moment. She'd been so sure that her idea would work! "Could you make some more pink ink?" she asked, thinking frantically. "How long would it take?"

Octavius nodded excitedly. "I could make some more ink if I was really happy, or laughing," he replied. "So if you can think of something funny . . ."

Marissa frowned in thought, but Rosie grinned; she had suddenly remembered the joke book she'd been reading back in the castle. "How about this?" she said. "Octavius, what is the most valuable fish in the world?"

Octavius shrugged. "I don't know," he said. "All fish are pretty special, so—"

Rosie interrupted him quickly. "The answer is . . . a *goldf*ish!"

Octavius broke off from his sentence and smiled. "Oh, it was a joke!" he said. "I love jokes."

"Great!" Rosie said. "Tell me, why are fish so clever?"

Octavius scratched his head with a tentacle. "I don't know. Why *are* fish so clever?" he asked after a moment.

"Because they live in schools!" Rosie replied.

Octavius chuckled. "I like that. They live in schools! I'll have to remember that one!"

Marissa joined in. "I've got one! A really good one!" she said excitedly. "Octavius, how come fish always know how much they weigh?"

Octavius shook his head. "I don't know."

"Because they have their own scales!"

Marissa replied, grinning.

Octavius laughed out loud. "Oh, that's a good one!" he said. "Have their own scales – very funny!" He grinned. "I think I've nearly got enough ink now," he told Rosie. "Do you want to pass me the seaweed, and try one more joke?"

Rosie gave Octavius the bundle of seaweed and thought quickly. "How can you tell if the ocean is friendly?" she asked. "Because it waves!"

Octavius burst out laughing, harder than ever. He clutched the seaweed tightly to himself and started squirting out his ink and spinning around so fast that he was soon just a blur of pink. Then, after a few moments, he slowed down and handed back the bundle of seaweed. It was bright pink!

"You did it!" Rosie cheered, throwing her

arms around the octopus.

"We *all* did it!" Octavius corrected her happily.

Marissa's eyes were shining as she hugged both Octavius and Rosie. "Thank you, Octavius. Thank you, Rosie. I think you've got me my crown back!"

Chapter Ten

"Let's go back and see Myrtle," Rosie said. "Thanks, Octavius!"

"Pleasure," Octavius said, waving them off, still chuckling. "Thanks for the jokes!"

Rosie and Marissa turned tail and headed back to Myrtle's cave.

The old mermaid answered on the first knock, and her eyes sparkled with happiness when she saw the pretty pink seaweed in Rosie's arms. "It's so beautiful!" she cried, examining it with delight. "I'll be able to knit something really special with this now," she beamed.

The water around them seemed to

shimmer with a strange golden light and
Rosie suddenly realized that, for the first time
since she'd met Myrtle, the sea near the old
mermaid wasn't freezing cold. She couldn't
help wondering if it was because Myrtle was
happier – she hoped so!

"A deal's a deal," Myrtle said, fetching
Marissa's crown and handing it to her.
"There you are, my dear."

Marissa put the crown back on her head.
"I am so glad to have this back," she said
thankfully. "That will be the end of any silly
decisions – I hope!"

Myrtle suddenly looked rather shy. "Well,
it's been lovely to have some company," she
said, a little longingly, "but you should
probably head home soon, before your
parents start worrying."

"You're right," Marissa said, also sounding
reluctant. Then she brightened. "Myrtle,

would you like to come back to the palace with us? That way I can introduce you to everyone. I want the whole kingdom to know how you helped us."

Myrtle gave a pleased little smile. "I'd love to come," she said. "Thank you."

Rosie, Marissa and Myrtle swam to the palace together. They found the king and queen in the grounds, making plans for a lavish rockery with all the stones that had arrived for the swimming pool.

"Can't imagine what got into me," the king was saying in a baffled voice. "Swimming pool! What was I thinking?"

Marissa coughed rather guiltily. "I think I can explain," she said. "You see, I lost the Pearl of Wisdom, which is why none of us were thinking very wisely. But Rosie helped me look for the crown. And Myrtle here," she said, drawing forward the old mermaid, "found it for me and kept it safe."

"Oh, thank goodness the pearl wasn't lost for ever!" the queen said in relief. She beamed at Myrtle and Rosie. "Thank you so much. Without the pearl, we would have continued to be very silly indeed!"

"Myrtle, did you say?" the king asked. "Much obliged. Very grateful! I think this calls for a celebratory banquet – with Myrtle and Rosie as our guests of honour!"

Before the banquet began, Rosie, Marissa and Myrtle went to meet the royal stylists to help choose their party clothes. "These shawls are fabulous!" squealed Angelica, one of the stylists, as soon as they came into the dressing room. "Where did you get them?"

"Myrtle made them," Rosie said, smiling at the old mermaid, who was blushing furiously.

"Darling, they are sen-sational," Coralie, the other stylist cooed, coming over to look at them more closely. "I must put in an order immediately!"

"So soft!" Angelica marvelled, running a finger down Rosie's shawl.

"And so well-made," Coralie chimed in, peering at the neat stitches on Marissa's. "Myrtle, you are very talented!"

"Thank you," Myrtle said, looking pleased and embarrassed all at the same time.

After looking at Myrtle's knitting, the stylists set to work finding some wonderful party clothes for the banquet. For Rosie, they picked out a cream-coloured halter-neck top embroidered with tiny glittery shells in all the colours of the rainbow. "It'll look divine with that shawl of yours," Angelica said approvingly.

For Marissa, they found a pink strappy top and some sparkly shell earrings. And for Myrtle, they chose a floaty plum-coloured top and pinned her hair up in an elegant top-knot.

When they were all ready, Rosie, Marissa and Myrtle swam down to the great hall to find the celebrations in full swing. Carla, Carlos and Octavius were already there, dancing together, as a trio of glamorous mermaids sang along to the merry tunes of the Underwater Orchestra.

Marissa began introducing Rosie and Myrtle to everyone – and they *all* wanted to know where Rosie and Marissa's gorgeous shawls had come from!

"Wait until you see my new pink range," Myrtle told the crowd of mermaids happily. She winked at Rosie and Marissa. "I think it's going to be my best work yet!"

"Oh, really?" Marissa's cousin, Kyla, said eagerly. "I can't wait to see it!"

After a delicious meal and lots of dancing with Marissa and her friends, Rosie knew that the time had come to leave. She swam

over to hug Myrtle and say goodbye.

"Take care, Rosie," the old mermaid replied, smiling. "Thanks to you and Marissa, I've made lots of new friends. I'm even thinking of opening a knitwear shop closer to the centre of Aquatica!"

Rosie went to say goodbye to Octavius next. She found him telling one of her jokes to Carlos and Carla. She hugged them all goodbye, and then she swam over to Marissa.

"Marissa, I've had so much fun with you, but I really have to go home now," Rosie said, feeling a little sad.

Marissa threw her arms around Rosie's neck. "Thank you for everything, Rosie," she said. "You're a friend of the mer-people for life now. Please come and see us again soon!"

"I will," Rosie promised. "Goodbye!"

As soon as the word had left her mouth,

the water around her
began to bubble and
a whirlpool formed.
Everything blurred in
front of her eyes, and
she felt a strange
tingling sensation in
her mermaid tail.
Seconds later, the
whirling slowed,
and Rosie opened
her eyes to find
herself back in the
castle garden, in
front of the fountain once more.

Rosie stared down at her legs and
kicked them out experimentally in front
of her, one after the other. It felt very
peculiar to have legs again, after swimming
with her wonderful mermaid tail!

"I told you! I told you!" came a voice just then.

Rosie looked round to see Luke racing across the garden towards her.

"Didn't I tell you that there really were mermaids?" he demanded excitedly.

Rosie grinned at her brother. "You know, I think Great-aunt Rosamund was right: there *are* mermaids," she agreed. "And I think they live in a hidden kingdom at the bottom of the ocean, and their existence has to be kept a secret." She gazed up at the mermaid statue and smiled. *And that,* she added in her head, *is all I'm going to tell you, Luke Campbell. A promise is a promise, after all!*

THE END

Did you enjoy reading about
Rosie's adventure with the Sea Princesss?
If you did, you'll love the next
Little Princesses
book!

Turn over to read the first chapter of
The Golden Princess.

Chapter One

"Luke! Where are you?"

Rosie hurried into the Great Hall of the castle and looked around, but her brother was nowhere in sight. He was probably playing in his bedroom, she decided. She went over to the wide oak staircase and skipped up the stairs.

Rosie hurried down the landing and up the spiral staircase that led to the top of of the castle's turrets. Luke's bedroom door was firmly closed, which Rosie thought rather strange. When Luke was playing, he and his toys usually spilled out of his

room onto the landing.

"Luke!" she called, rapping on the big wooden door. "Mum wants to know if you want a sandwich."

"Oh!" Luke replied, sounding startled and a little bit guilty. "Just a minute, Rosie!"

Rosie frowned and put her ear to the door. She could hear lots of shuffling coming from the other side. He's up to something! she thought, and flung the door open.

Luke was sitting on the floor surrounded by a jumble of toy cars. He almost jumped out of his skin when Rosie marched in. Quickly he scrambled to his feet, biting his lip.

"What's going on?" asked Rosie suspiciously.

"I didn't mean to do it!" Luke said anxiously.

"Do what?" Rosie asked.

Slowly Luke knelt down and slid his hand under the bed to pull out two dazzling pieces of curved golden metal.

"I found this in my room ages ago," he explained miserably, handing the metal pieces to Rosie. "But I accidentally broke it. I think it's some kind of necklace."

Rosie's eyes opened wide with surprise as she examined the metal. "It is a kind of necklace," she agreed. "It's called a torque." She glanced sternly at Luke. "How did you break it?"

She glanced sternly at Luke. "How did you break it?"

"I was using it as a ramp for my toy cars," Luke muttered. "It was great because it's curved and really smooth, but then it snapped and I can't put it back together."

Rosie weighed the pieces of the torque in her hand. It was so heavy, she was sure it was solid gold. Then she looked more closely at the place where it had snapped. Suddenly a smile spread across her face. "Luke, it isn't broken!" she announced. "Look, it's supposed to come apart so that you can get it on and off more easily!"

"Really?" Luke gasped, his face lighting up with relief.

Rosie nodded. It took her a few minutes, but eventually she managed to slot the two pieces together. There was a snap as they slid into place.

"Brilliant!" Luke exclaimed.

"But no more using it as a car ramp," Rosie said with a grin. "I'll put it in Mum and Dad's room."

"OK," replied Luke, bouncing over to the door with all his usual energy. "I'll go and have my sandwich now."

When Luke had gone, Rosie went down to her parents' bedroom, carrying the torque carefully. She put it down on the dressing table but couldn't tear her eyes away from the beautiful necklace. It was engraved with delicate patterns, and at one end she saw the figure of a sad-looking girl wearing a long dress and a crown. "It's a little princess!" Rosie gasped.

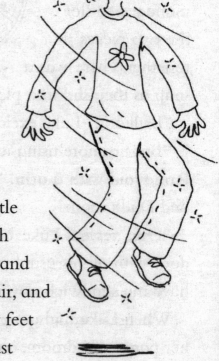

She bobbed a curtsey, just as her great-aunt had told her to. "Hello!" she said softly.

Immediately a gentle breeze swirled through the room. It felt cool and crisp, like mountain air, and it swept Rosie off her feet as flecks of golden dust danced around her and the smell of lush green grass filled her nostrils.

I wonder where I'm going this time, Rosie thought, closing her eyes and remembering all her previous exciting adventures.

Seconds later the breeze died away and Rosie felt herself land lightly on the ground. She opened her eyes and looked around eagerly to see that she was standing in a green valley between two mountains, under a deep blue sky.

THUD!

Rosie jumped as an enormous block of grey stone crashed down right beside her. It was so enormous, it made the ground under her feet tremble. "Oh!" she gasped, leaping aside. "Where did *that* come from?"

She glanced up and, to her amazement, saw a huge stone figure, towering above her.

It's a *giant*! Rosie thought, her heart

thumping with terror. And that wasn't just a block of stone – it was his *foot*!

She gazed up at the giant in awe. He seemed to be made entirely of dark rock and there was moss and lichen growing on his head and chin. His face was angular and his eyes were deep set. Rosie thought that he looked sad. But she had no time to consider it because at that moment the stone giant lifted his other foot, and she watched in horror as it started to come down right over her head.

Read the rest of *The Golden Princess* to find out what happens to Rosie!

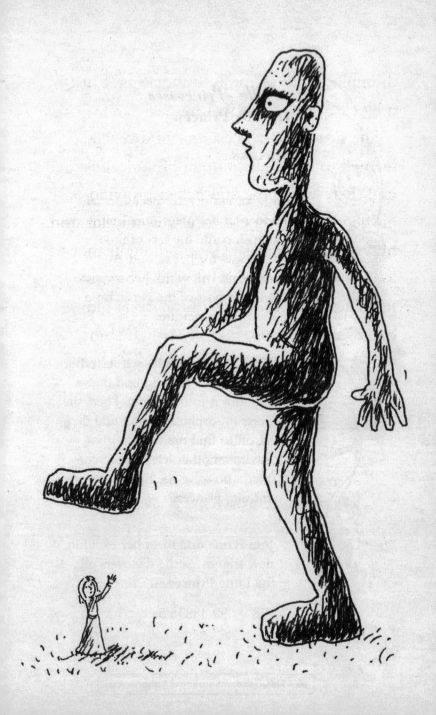

Little Princesses
The Silk Princess

Katie Chase

Rosie knows a very special secret. Hidden in her great-aunt's mysterious Scottish castle are lots of little princesses for her to find. And each one will whisk her away to another part of the world on a magical adventure!

When Rosie finds herself in India, the princess is missing and the kingdom is in mourning. Then, she meets an orphan, Suvita, and they set off to find the treasure that Suvita's mother left her, but can they also solve the mystery of the missing princess?

Join Rosie and meet her exciting new friends, as she discovers all the Little Princesses.

978 0 099 48838 5

www.kidsatrandomhouse.co.uk/littleprincesses